TURNER STREET

Where the Monsters in the Closet are Real

Books by R.S. Veira

Turner Street: The Cain Seed

Turner Street: Anomalies

The Last Guardians (Tales of Aela Book One)

Dream With Me: A Dreamer's Ramblings on Life, Love, God, and Achieving the Dream

TURNER STREET

Where the Monsters in the Closet are Real

Turner Street Chronicles Book I

R.S. Veira

RSV Ink
An Imprint of Dream With Me Productions

TURNER STREET: Where the Monsters in the Closet are Real

RSV Ink 2nd Edition 2021

Published by RSV Ink
Los Angeles, California

Cover design by Laurie Wright
https://www.fiverr.com/lauria

Edited by Vince Font (Glass Spider Publishing)
https://www.glassspiderpublishing.com

RSV Ink books may be purchased for educational, business, or sales promotional use. For information please e-mail RSV Ink at RSVInkbooks@dwmprod.com

Dream With Me Productions Website: https://www.dwmprod.com

FIRST RSV INK PAPERBACK EDITION PUBLISHED IN 2021

Library of Congress Control Number: 2021910099

ISBN 978-1-7369742-0-9

EPUB ISBN 978-1-7369742-1-6

For Papa, who always checked my closet.

TABLE OF CONTENTS

PROLOGUE

The following pages are home to a collection of stories documenting the unusual events that have befallen Turner Street. The demons confined to the nook in our imaginations—imprisoned by the arbitrary belief that they do not exist, pressed upon us by parents who grew weary of checking our closets—have no such restraints here. Turner Street is a place where the line between reality and fantasy is no more real than those on a map and few things, if any, can be explained. Here are the stories from those who walk Turner Street's sidewalks, reside in its closets, and tremble in its beds.

Welcome to Turner Street…

1428 Turner Street:

Agent Jericho

Jericho wiped the thin layer of dust from his eyes and gently wiggled free from Amelia's strangling embrace. He stretched and waddled over the lumps in the bed until he reached the edge. It was his first night on patrol in the house at 1428 Turner Street, and he was bent on ensuring his charge survived the night.

Against his better judgment, he allowed himself to glance over his shoulder at the sleeping child. Few things were more precious, but the sight of this slumbering angel only reminded him of the one he had failed. He shook his head, buried the pain, and dammed up the flood of emotions it was itching to trigger.

He jumped from the bed and somersaulted as he hit

the ground. He rolled a few inches before righting himself and continuing on toward a heap of toys sitting at the base of the wall opposite Amelia's bed.

He riffled through the pile, tossing aside jacks, Legos, dolls, and the like until he found a small black satchel. From within it, he withdrew his badge. *IWPS* was embossed prominently on the front, and printed underneath were the words *Special Agent.*

The gravity of his current situation was not lost on him. The unusual occurrences on Turner Street over the last few years had been well documented by the Invisible World Protective Service (IWPS). The death the previous night of Amelia's last protector, Special Agent Thomas Williams, signaled that things were only going to escalate. The IWPS did its best to squash any demon that threatened the life of a child. Any sign of weakness on the IWPS's behalf would lead to the fall of human civilization. At least that was the line they fed their agents.

Like Agent Williams before him, Jericho was one of the few agents in the IWPS willing to take on the appearance of a teddy bear, and because of this, he was the logical replacement. Jericho had received his assignment early that morning. Amelia's file was thicker than most novels. She was, for all intents and purposes, a high-profile case. She had been the target of a bizarrely high number of otherworldly attacks, many of which were thwarted by Agent Williams—until the one that had resulted in his death.

Luckily, before he died, Williams had managed to jam the closet door shut until morning, saving Amelia.

Jericho could relate. However, in his case, he had survived and his charge was taken. Nonetheless, this case would be different. He would not lose another child.

He continued shifting through the contents of his satchel until he came across his cardboard sword and scabbard. The sword was encrusted with a thick layer of applesauce and melted sugar, which happened to be a devastating combination when fighting the demons that hunted children.

Besides the children themselves–whom demons found *delicious*–they despised all things having to do with the innocence and sweetness that comes with childhood. If used properly, these items could inflict heavy damage. Jericho pinned his badge to his furry chest, wrapped his sword and scabbard around his waist, and slung his satchel over his shoulder.

It was then that he heard the closet door near Amelia's bed creak open. He whirled around. Four exceptionally sharp claws attached to four impossibly long scaly fingers extended from the darkness of the closet.

Jericho sprinted for the bed. "No!" he screamed.

It was happening again. He could hear his previous charge's cries for help as he was dragged away into the darkness. But this time, the demon's hand hesitated for a moment, and that was all Jericho needed. He lunged onto the bed, landing softly on Amelia's stomach, facing the closet. He drew his sword and aimed it at the intruder's outstretched arm.

"I am Special Agent Jericho of the IWPS. This child is under my protection. No harm will come to her!"

The beast snarled. It nudged the closet door open so its head was in full view. Its massive cranium was double the size of Jericho's body. He likened its flat head to that of a lizard. Its red eyes locked with Jericho's black plastic ones. Its powerful jaw hung open, showing off rows of prickly teeth. Saliva flowed freely from both sides of its mouth and pooled on the carpet.

"Demon!" Jericho roared. "There will be no feast tonight!"

The beast's arm shot forward, but Jericho was far too quick. He sidestepped the attack and brought down his sword with all his might, cutting deep into the beast's flesh. It howled in pain and retracted its arm.

Jericho charged forward. The beast retreated into the closet, frantically waving its injured arm to defend itself. One of its desperate swipes caught Jericho across the chest, and puffs of cotton spilled from the wound and onto the bed. Jericho paid it no mind. Amelia's safety was his sole concern.

He soared above the bed and swung his sword at the beast's naked hand. The blade made contact with one of its claws and sliced through with little resistance. With that, the demon fully retreated into the darkness.

While still in the air, Jericho pulled two marble-shaped grenades from his satchel. He tossed them into the closet and slammed the door shut with his shoulder. There were two faint *pops* as the grenades exploded, followed by the muffled moans of his defeated adversary.

Jericho landed on his back near the severed claw. He got up and kicked it under the bed. That was work for the cleanup crew. His world and this war were referred to as "invisible" for a reason. There was never any evidence.

He climbed back on top of the bed and collected the pieces of cotton that had fallen from his chest, then reached into his satchel to retrieve a needle and thread to mend his wound.

"She's safe," Jericho sighed—but, as it usually goes with these things, the moment the words left his mouth, the closet door was again ajar and two yellow eyes had settled on him. He tucked his needle and thread into his satchel and rose with his sword in hand.

The night had just begun.

1431 Turner Street:

Lucius's Gift

A school bus came to a halt at 1431 Turner Street, and its final passenger disembarked. Lucius hopped from the bus and into the afternoon sun. Its rays rejuvenated his drained batteries. The weekend had arrived right on time. The daily grind of structured education had taken its toll. High school had a way of making him feel more like a prisoner than anything else. He stretched his arms wide, savoring his temporary freedom, all the while relishing the sound of the departing bus.

He strolled up his driveway humming "Get Down on It" by Kool & the Gang, the last song he'd heard on the bus's radio. It was way before his time, but the rhythm was intoxicating. So much so that he lost himself in his own imitation of it and tripped on the large brown box sitting at his door. He quickly regained his balance and surveyed the street for any witnesses. There was only one person in sight: a little girl across the street. However, her back was to him and her focus was on the teddy bear in her hands.

Lucius's attention was again on the brown box, whose existence was peculiar. He and his mother never ordered anything, be it online, by mail, or over the phone. His mother had a tremendous fear of deliverymen caused by a supposed break-in shortly after his birth.

As the story went, when Lucius was a toddler, his mother left him alone for roughly twenty minutes—according to her—in order to run to the store. She returned to find a man standing over his crib who vanished by the time she fetched the phone to dial the authorities.

Her theory was built on the idea that a deliveryman had watched as she left and seized the opportunity. She deduced that while she ran to get the phone, he had leaped from Lucius's bedroom window.

Lucius was a little more skeptical; his mother was known to take back one too many glasses of wine. To say her drinking was out of control would be polite. It was something he had come to resent her for. It was far more likely that she'd simply imagined the situation while intoxicated. Either way, it was impossible for him not to look at delivery trucks and their short-shorted drivers with a wary eye.

After further inspection, Lucius found no return address, only his name and his own address neatly printed in the upper-right corner. He gave it a light kick and a soft *thud* echoed up to his ears. His curiosity was piqued. He scooped up the package and marched inside.

He didn't expect his mother to be home for a couple of hours, which granted him absolute privacy. He sat down at the dinner table with the box in front of him and pried the lid apart. He was greeted by a white envelope with the letters IWPS embossed in the center. It rested on top of the green packing peanuts that filled the box. He tossed it aside and plunged both hands into the sea of peanuts. His right hand grasped what felt like a remote. He withdrew his hands and in his right palm sat what could best be described as a calculator.

"You have to be kidding me," he murmured.

He overturned the box, emptying it entirely, but there was nothing more. The edge of the white envelope he had tossed aside protruded just enough from the mountain of packing peanuts to catch his eye. He ripped it open and read the letter within:

The time machine inside is yours to do with as you please. If you want to learn how to properly utilize it, come visit me on this date: 01.15.2055.

Plug the numbers in as printed and press Enter. I eagerly await your arrival.

– A dear friend

Lucius knew better than to take things at face value. When he was five, his father told Lucius he was going to the toy store to buy him a new set of Legos. That was eleven years ago, and he had yet to return.

Yet something about today was different. It may have been because it was the weekend or that he had nothing better to do, but he decided to indulge the letter. He stood up and plugged 01.15.2055 into the time machine and pressed Enter. A blue light on the corner of the device began to flash repeatedly. In an instant, he was encapsulated in an opaque blue sphere, but just as fast as it came, the sphere was gone. The device chimed, and

Lucius stood in what appeared to be the same house, but now an older gentleman sat across from him at the dinner table.

Lucius glared at the intruder. "What are you doing in my house?!"

"I should be asking you the same question," the man chuckled. "Sit down, Lucius."

A familiar tone in the man's voice soothed his nerves, and he did as he was told. "Are you the one who sent me this?" Lucius waved the time machine in his hand.

"Yes, I've been waiting for you."

"Who are you?"

"I'm you. I thought that much was obvious," the man laughed.

"No, it's not *obvious*," Lucius said, but he had to admit the man's banshee-like laugh was eerily similar to his own, if not dead on. "What the hell is going on?"

Lucius's gaze journeyed along the lines on the old man's face, and more similarities became apparent. They shared the same almond eyes and untidy brown hair. But it was the birthmark that ran down the man's neck that compelled Lucius to gently caress his own.

The old man smiled. "It's one heck of a birthmark. I

like to think it's one of a kind."

"My thoughts exactly," Lucius responded.

"It's good to know you got the time machine," the old man continued.

"But how?" Lucius asked.

"That I have yet to completely figure out, but at your age, I received the same gift from myself."

"But how is that *possible*?"

The old man sighed. "I can't give you all the answers now. You're not ready, believe me, I would know. But you will get them in due time. I *can* tell you that you must send it back to our past self, prior to or on January 15th, 2055."

"Why's that?"

"Because if we don't send it back, then how will we get it?"

"I guess if anything, that makes sense. So what can I do with it?"

"Anything—well, at least anything between the time when we first received it and when we send it back—is open for our manipulation. So you have about forty years to play with. You can visit outside those parameters, but if you aren't careful, it can have serious consequences."

"Like what?"

Old Lucius's eyes caught his younger self's stare. "Time travel is messy. Even I don't know all the rules, and I've had that machine for decades. But you need to know this. The 'deliveryman' who broke into the house all those years ago was us. One of us went too far back and allowed Mom to see us, which led to her relying a little more on the bottle and blaming Dad for her, uh, lost sense of security. After a while, that pushed him out the door."

They were both silent for a while. Young Lucius rubbed his throbbing temples. "Alright. So it was my fault after all. I suppose *I* owe them an apology."

"Indeed."

"Why didn't you just fix it?"

"Because, as I said, time travel is messy and I didn't want to make it worse. Each time we jump and change something, we create an alternate timeline."

Lucius nodded. "Okay. So if I have it now, what are you going to do?"

"Who knows? I never traveled farther than this. I wanted to experience things for the first time again. You'd be surprised how time travel loses its novelty after a while."

"We'll see," young Lucius chuckled but suddenly stopped. "How did you manage to send this back to me and return to your own time?"

Old Lucius gave a weary smile. "This machine will open doors to worlds you didn't even know existed. The people you find there will have all the answers you need."

Young Lucius nodded. "Well…thanks, man." With that, he punched in a date and was gone in a flash of blue light.

1451 Turner Street:

Agent Benjamin's Inspection

Agent Benjamin pulled up in front of a neat one-story home at 1451 Turner Street, turned off his car, and sat in near silence. The only sound came from the squeaking of his sweaty brown hands nervously rubbing against the steering wheel. This was one of the rare assignments where he found himself without a partner. His superiors had assured him it was nothing more than a routine check-in on a rehabilitated criminal. There was nothing to worry about.

He had to agree, for the most part. Based on the demon's peaceful activity over the last few decades, this was a low-risk assignment. Nonetheless, he never felt comfortable without backup, and unfortunately his most recent partner had been reassigned to a more pressing case, which coincidentally was up the street at 1428.

"At least he's in the neighborhood," Benjamin sighed. "As if that means anything."

He glanced at his hands, which were throttling the wheel, and a small smile spread across his face. One of the few perks of this assignment was that he got to take on human form. A privilege he never took for granted. While in the human world, agents of the Invisible World Protective Service and demons could assume any form they wished. The only stipulation being they had to abide by the laws of that form. Most chose to be humans since they were capable of feeling and experiencing things that neither agents nor demons could. Benjamin had taken the appearance of a slim, bald African-American male.

Benjamin finally managed to pry his hands from the steering wheel and flipped through the demon's file once more. It was hard to ignore the fact that when this demon had been at large, it had committed numerous murders and even more kidnappings. In this regard, his superior's votes of confidence did little to settle his anxiety. Yet, despite his uneasiness, it was his duty as an agent to uphold the treaty between the IWPS and the demons of the Underworld. According to said treaty, demons were permitted to stay in the human world as long as they didn't bring harm to any of the inhabitants. Compared to their regular living conditions, it was paradise—but if they violated the treaty, they were either killed on the spot or imprisoned for however long the IWPS felt necessary. Upon their release, they were monitored and regularly checked on.

Benjamin was not a fan of the latter part of the system. He would much rather rid the human world of demons altogether, but even a hint of such an act would cause a full-scale war—something neither side wanted since it would be fought on human soil. Once killed there, agents and demons ceased to exist. There was no afterlife for them. That was a pleasure reserved for the humans. That fact was at the heart of demon hatred toward humanity, and the reason the IWPS fought desperately to protect them. Humans had no say on whether to be born into such a privilege.

Benjamin had to concede that even though things weren't perfect, they were manageable. Of course there were hiccups, such as the fiasco in Germany when a demon managed to rise to power causing worldwide chaos or the "Ripper" in London. But no system was perfect, and as long as the IWPS allowed for some demons to stay among the humans, the powers that be in the Underworld kept the most dangerous ones there.

He pulled his badge from his pocket and pinned it to his suit jacket. He took one last deep breath, grabbed his briefcase, and left the car.

The house before him was by no means threatening. In fact, it was inviting. The manicured lawn and immaculate flower arrangements were more along the lines of a welcoming neighbor than a convicted murderer. He rang the doorbell and in a matter of seconds was greeted by a petite old woman. Her pale skin sagged from her cheeks, and deep wrinkles ran rampant along her face. Her gray, curly hair fell just below her ears. At a glance she was nonthreatening, but her vibrant green eyes put Benjamin on edge. They were sharp and focused, too much so for a woman of her age.

"Ms…" Benjamin's mind blanked.

"Ms. Hemmings, Officer," she nodded at his badge.

"Of course, Mary Anne Hemmings." Benjamin shook his head. "I'm sorry, it slipped my mind. Anyway, you know why I'm here, just checking in."

"Yes, it is about that time, isn't it?" Mary Anne smiled. Her teeth were crooked and yellow. "Well, come in, let's get this over with. Is it just you?"

"Yes."

Benjamin brushed past and into the small home. From his vantage point, most of the house's layout was visible. The living room he stood in was connected to the dining room, which was in turn connected to the kitchen, and beyond that he assumed were the bedroom and bathroom. He quickly scanned the living room and took a few steps toward the coffee table in the center but stopped dead. A putrid stench assaulted his nostrils.

"What's that smell?"

"Some of the beef I use for my chili went bad," she laughed. "I forgot to put it up last night."

"I see," Benjamin continued onward. "I read in your file that your chili is pretty famous."

"Yes, sir, thirteen-time winner at the county fair. I have the ribbons to prove it." She pointed at a wall in her living room coated in framed ribbons.

"I see."

"You should try a bowl."

"If you pass the inspection…I'll consider it." Benjamin placed his briefcase on the coffee table and opened it. He withdrew a pair of infrared glasses and a small crossbow. A thick, short arrow was already loaded, its tip coated in applesauce and melted sugar.

"There will be no need for that," Ms. Hemmings said.

"We will see," Benjamin responded. "As you know, according to the treaty, if I discover any human blood or remains on the premises, your probation will be terminated immediately and I have the right to kill you on the spot. Understood?"

She smiled, revealing all of her dirty teeth. "Understood, but Officer, I assure you it will not come to that."

Benjamin said nothing more. He began his inspection in the living room then proceeded into the dining room, kitchen, and then down a short hallway which led to the bedroom and bathroom, respectively. He finally returned to the living room to find Ms. Hemmings sitting by her coffee table with a bowl of chili resting beside his briefcase.

"All clear," Benjamin said. He sat down across from the old woman and returned his glasses to his briefcase. He kept his crossbow in his lap.

"I told you. So, how about that bowl of chili?"

Benjamin's shoulders sagged, and he leaned back into his chair. "I don't see why not." He picked up the bowl and began eating. Slowly at first, but within minutes the bowl was clean. "I see why you won thirteen years in a row." Benjamin smiled.

Ms. Hemmings returned the smile. "It's all about finding the right ingredients."

"I believe it. You know, I wasn't sure what to expect when I first arrived, your file is pretty thick. It's good to know that the rehabilitation program is actually working." Benjamin took a deep breath and immediately wrinkled his face. His nostrils had again been stricken by that putrid smell.

"You really need to do something about—" Benjamin stopped speaking. His vision blurred and his head ached.

Ms. Hemmings chuckled. "I didn't think the tranquilizers would affect you so fast."

"Tranq—" Benjamin's mouth went numb.

"Don't try to speak, sweetie, there's no point now. In

a few minutes, you'll be out. You might as well go in peace."

Benjamin tried to reach for his crossbow but despite his pleas, his arms did nothing. He unwillingly slumped farther into his seat, all strength leaving him. Ms. Hemmings rose and moved the coffee table off the rug it was sitting on. She pulled back the rug and revealed a trapdoor.

"No matter what I do, the scent from the leftover meat never fades," she shrugged.

She pulled open the trapdoor and a rancid odor engulfed the room. She then ambled over and squatted in front of Benjamin.

"You know, it's ironic. The same crime that the IWPS nearly killed me for, has made me a local celebrity." She held up the empty chili bowl. "Now you understand why we go to such lengths to get human flesh. It's delicious when prepared correctly."

She grabbed Benjamin by the ankles and dragged him toward the trapdoor. "I'm tired of hiding, Benjamin. Thankfully, I won't have to much longer. A war is coming, but I guess that doesn't concern you anymore, now, does it?"

She pushed his limp body through the opening in the floor. Benjamin landed on his back. His vision continued to blur as Ms. Hemmings descended the ladder which led to her hidden lair.

"You know what, Benjamin? I think you'll win me my fourteenth ribbon."

1450 Turner Street:
The Brody Twins

Aron couldn't remember a time when he wasn't able to hear his sister's thoughts in his head. It seemed as if they had shared the same brain since birth. So naturally, he found it troubling when he suddenly realized it was his thoughts alone bouncing around in his noggin. He took a break from his Game Boy to see his twin sister, Samantha, motionless as she gazed out their bedroom window. Unsettled, Aron probed her mind to find the reason for her silence. Somehow, her thoughts were still hidden from him. He was forced to do what the Brody twins rarely did: speak aloud.

"I thought we didn't hide anything," Aron said. There was no response. Aron put down his Game Boy, cleared his throat, and tried again. "Sam, are you okay? Why can't I hear you?"

"There's something wrong, Aron," Samantha responded, while still peering through the window.

Aron rose from his bean bag and approached. He stood slightly behind her and glared over her shoulder.

"There's nothing there, it's just Ms. Hemmings's house," Aron said.

"You see that car?" Samantha pointed at the parked car in the driveway of 1451 Turner Street.

"What about it?"

"It hasn't moved in weeks."

"So? She hasn't left her house in a while. That doesn't explain why I can't hear your thoughts."

"It's not her car, Aron. I saw when the man pulled up. I saw him go in and never come out."

They both stood in silence. "I didn't think much of it at first," Samantha continued. "I assumed it was her son or something. But when I saw her move the car from the street to her driveway, I knew something was wrong. I've just been thinking of all the possibilities, and I didn't want to alarm you."

Aron gently took hold of her shoulders and turned her around so she faced him. He took her hands and held them in his.

Aron smiled. "It's okay. It's just…I've never had my thoughts to myself. I was kinda lonely."

Samantha let out a forced laugh, but her eyes remained intense. Aron was a bit taller, so he had to look down to make eye contact. They shared the same pale skin, black hair, and green eyes. His hair was an unkempt mess while hers rested neatly on her shoulders. Despite being fraternal, they were nearly identical.

Aron tightened his grip around Samantha's hands. "Remember, together we can do anything."

Aron let go of her left hand and pointed at his bean bag. It slowly rose into the air, and as Aron's finger danced, it followed suit. Samantha wiggled free of Aron's other hand, and the bean bag dropped to the floor.

"I know, Aron…"

"Then what's wrong?"

"We need to help."

"Help who? And how? For all we know, it really was her son. And anyway, we just turned *twelve…last week-*

end. This is a problem for the grown-ups."

Samantha grabbed one of his hands and pointed at his Game Boy. It, too, floated in the air. "Together we can do anything."

Aron shook his head. "Okay. We'll check out the house, but we have to agree to never close our minds to one another again." He paused for a moment. "Well…at least everything but our most private thoughts."

Samantha laughed. "Agreed."

The Brody twins snuck past their parents, who were watching TV in the den, strolled across the street, and tiptoed up to Ms. Hemmings's back window.

Aron stood on his toes and peered inside. "I can't see a thing, I need a boost," he whispered.

Samantha extended her arm. "Take my hand."

They locked fingers and concentrated. Their feet slowly left the ground as they began to levitate.

"Not too high," Aron hissed.

Once both their eyes cleared the windowsill, they stopped. The house was empty.

"I don't see anyone," Samantha's thoughts echoed in Aron's head.

*"Me either…it's nice to hear your **real** voice again,"* Aron responded.

"Likewise, but what should we do?"

A bright flash of blue light erupted from behind them. They dropped back down to the ground and spun around. A boy, a few years older than them, was waiting. He had a strange birthmark on his neck, and Aron noticed him quickly tuck what looked like a calculator into his front pocket.

"I don't have time to explain, but we need to leave *now*," the boy said, his tone stern but calm.

The twins said nothing at first. "That's strange. I can't read your thoughts," Samantha said.

"Because you taught me how to hide them. If we don't go now, we will all die."

The twins looked at each other and nodded. "Okay, let's go."

The boy turned, sprinted down the driveway and then down the street. The twins followed. They finally stopped in front of 1428 Turner Street.

"Why are we at Amelia's house?" Aron asked.

"Because we need Jericho," the boy said, walking to the front door.

"Who?" the twins asked in unison.

"No one named Jericho lives here. Amelia is in our class, she's an only child," Aron said.

The boy continued toward the house without saying a word. Aron grabbed his sister's hand and pointed. The boy stopped dead in his tracks and was lifted into the air. Aron twirled his finger and spun him around.

"We followed you here, but we won't go anywhere else unless you explain."

"Fine…My name is Lucius, and I live across the street at 1431."

"I knew he looked familiar," Samantha said under her breath.

"Everything I'm going to tell you is the truth, but I'm only going to say this once. It all started when I first followed you guys to that house. I always thought Ms. Hemmings was weird, and when I saw you guys going over to check things out, I decided I'd tag along to make sure nothing happened to you…" Lucius trailed off.

"What happened?" Samantha prodded.

"Things went bad, really bad. So I came back to fix it."

"What do you mean?" Samantha asked.

"I'm a time traveler. You two were right to suspect Ms. Hemmings of doing some weird stuff over there. The things she…*it's* doing are horrible. I know you two can read people's minds, and when you make contact with one another, you gain telekinesis. In a different timeline, Samantha taught me how to conceal my thoughts. She thought all this information may overwhelm you guys if I came back and you had free rein in my head."

Aron let go of his sister's hand, and Lucius dropped to the ground.

"Like I said, we're here to get Jericho's help. He's an agent from the IWPS."

"The what?" Aron asked.

"We don't have time for me to explain all that. You just have to trust me."

The twins said nothing aloud for a while. Finally, Aron spoke. "Why didn't you mention me when you talked about the future?"

Lucius averted his eyes. "Because in every timeline that I've lived through, you die in that house—but we've never tried this with Jericho."

Again, the twins said nothing.

"In the last timeline I was in," Lucius continued, "things ended differently. She not only killed Aron but captured Samantha, as well. I only escaped because of Jericho. He told me to come back and find him."

Aron nodded. "Take us to him."

Lucius walked to the front door, picked up the door-mat, and removed a hidden key. "Stay close. Amelia and her family shouldn't be back for a while, but every action we make changes the timeline, so just in case they do surprise us, we'll have to get out of here quickly."

Lucius led them through the house, up the stairs, and into the first bedroom on the left. The room was neatly put together except for a pile of toys in the corner. On top of that pile was a teddy bear. Lucius grabbed it and held it out toward the twins.

"This is Jericho."

"That's a teddy bear," Aron responded.

"Read its mind," Lucius insisted.

"That's a teddy bear," Aron repeated.

"No...he's right, Aron," Samantha whispered. "His name is Jericho, he's an agent in the Invisible World

Protective Service. His badge number is 3492. Agent Jericho, if I can call you that, we need your help."

To Aron's surprise, the teddy bear broke free from Lucius's grip and fell to the ground. It righted itself and glared up at them.

"Who are you?" it said. "And what do you want?"

"My name is Lucius, and these are the Brody twins. We need your help in stopping the demon that goes by the name of Mary Anne Hemmings."

The Battle of 1451 Turner Street (Part I)

Lucius patted his front pocket to make sure his time machine was indeed still there. He wouldn't dare venture any farther without it. He had relived their upcoming battle with Ms. Hemmings enough to know he would need it. He had witnessed the carnage unfold more times than he would ever admit to Jericho or the twins, and each time seemed to be worse than the last.

Even with the advantage time travel provided, he and the twins never seemed to have enough to take down the demon. But this time, it would be different. This time, they had Jericho.

Lucius cradled Jericho in his arms like a football and sprinted down Turner Street with the Brody twins in tow.

They stopped just before 1451. Lucius released Jericho, who seemed to almost float down to the concrete.

Jericho's black satchel hung from his shoulder, his sword rested in its scabbard by his side, and his IWPS badge was pinned to his furry chest. The children gathered around him, awaiting their orders. He glanced up at each one of them, but his eyes lingered on the twins.

"There's nothing I can say that will prepare you for what could happen in there," Jericho said.

"We understand…" Aron began.

"No, you don't. This is neither a movie nor a video game. This is real. If you die in there, it's over. There's no coming back."

Lucius cleared his throat. "That's not entirely true, Jericho."

"I'm assuming you're referring to your time machine?" Jericho responded.

"Yes, I can always go back. I can keep going back until we kill her and we all survive."

Jericho shook his head. "As you said before, no matter what you did, Aron always died in that house. You can't erase death. No matter how many times you go back, death will never change."

"So I'm doomed to die in there?"

Jericho turned his back to them and faced 1451, "Most likely."

"Not necessarily," Samantha said. "Jericho said we can't erase death. But there was only one death, so if Ms. Hemmings dies instead of Aron, couldn't she take his place?"

Jericho said nothing. "I wouldn't get your hopes up."

"You ordered me to come back in time to get you because you said you could help us!" Lucius exclaimed.

"I will help you, but I won't guarantee that if we all go in there, we all come out. That's just not the reality of the situation. I'm telling you this because this is no longer your fight. You don't have to follow me in there."

"You can't think we're going to let you go in alone," Samantha said.

"Once you informed me of Ms. Hemmings's crimes, it became *my duty* as an agent of the IWPS to put a stop to it. Not yours."

"You're a teddy bear," Aron responded. "No offense, but we're not going to leave this up to you."

Jericho gave no response and approached 1451.

Lucius shook his head, and Samantha shoved Aron. "For a telepath, you're pretty oblivious. Jericho isn't even trying to hide his thoughts from us. Take a look, he's more than qualified for this."

Aron was quiet for a while. "Yeah, you're right. But I don't think we should go in there anymore, Sam."

"We have to. You promised we would help, remember?"

"Yeah, that was before I knew I *died* in there."

"We don't know that for sure. Lucius said the timeline changes all the time. And imagine how many more she will kill if we do nothing."

Lucius began to follow Jericho before he stopped and turned back to the twins. "You guys really don't have to come. I wouldn't blame you. This really never was your fight."

"It isn't yours, either…so why are you going?" Aron asked.

"I don't know, but ever since I got this," Lucius tapped his front pocket, "I've realized things aren't always about me."

The twins stared at him. "Well, you came back not only to stop Ms. Hemmings but to save me," Aron said. "I guess I owe you. So we're coming too."

Samantha grabbed Aron's hand. "Yup."

By the time they caught up to Jericho, he had already pried open Ms. Hemmings's back window. He slipped in with the others right behind him. Lucius held his finger against his lips and pointed to the square trapdoor on the floor. She would be waiting for them down there.

"She knows we're here…she always does," Lucius whispered. "If we wait too long, she'll come up to us…but if we go right now, we might catch her by surprise."

"Unlikely," Jericho said flatly. "If she's as deadly as you claim, there is no catching her by surprise."

He lightly tapped the trapdoor. "I'll go down first. The twins will follow behind me, and Lucius, you come last."

They all nodded. "Lucius, on my command, lift the door." Jericho then pulled out what looked like three marbles from his satchel. "Now!"

Lucius flung the trapdoor open, and Jericho dove into the darkness. There were three small, distinct explosions followed by an unnatural howl of pain.

"You two ready?" Lucius asked.

"Yes," they answered in unison.

The twins stood up, and Aron's right hand interlocked with Samantha's left. They took a step and levitated over the opening. They then began a quick but controlled descent. Lucius waited a few moments, until their heads had disappeared from view, before he jumped in.

He fell into a cellar. The only light came from the fire in an open furnace in the corner. Next to the furnace was a long table decorated with chunks of flesh. At the end sat a pile of discarded clothes and a mountain of cleaned bones. However, this horrific sight did not hold Lucius's attention for long. It was quickly redirected toward the beast that was roaring in the middle of the room.

Ms. Hemmings, or what used to be Ms. Hemmings, scratched wildly at Jericho as he jumped and twirled about. The demon's thin, razor-sharp claws were attached to two lanky arms. Its body was obese. Its stomach nearly graced the floor. Its head was wide and bald. Its eyes bulged perversely from its head, and a large sack hung from its neck. It reminded Lucius of a frog.

The twins stood to the side of Lucius. Aron pointed at the beast, and it began to levitate. With the flick of his wrist, he sent it hurling into a wall. Jericho seized the opportunity. He dove on top of the beast's grotesque stomach and drew his sword. Unfortunately, the beast quickly recovered and one of its claws rifled through Jericho's chest. In spite of the claw protruding from his furry back, Jericho brought down his sword into the beast's exposed gut. Its deafening scream dripped with agony.

Aron raised his hand to offer further assistance but it was then that the sack attached to the beast's neck jiggled, and from the beast's mouth spewed a colorless liquid directed at the twins.

"Watch out!" Lucius yelled as he barreled into them. The twins were sent sprawling across the floor, their hands no longer intertwined. The liquid soared past and into the wall behind them.

"Acid..." Lucius hissed, pointing at a now-gaping hole in the wall.

"Ahhhhh!" Jericho screamed.

Lucius looked up in time to witness the beast cut off Jericho's leg and his sword-wielding arm. It then tossed him aside like a hand-me-down toy. He landed at the base of the mountain of bones.

"No!" Lucius yelled.

The beast paid no attention to Lucius's cries. Its jaw unhinged, and it showered Jericho in acid. Jericho's sharp screams cut through the stale cellar air and quickly became a gargled mess. Within seconds, the agent was no more.

Lucius reached for his front pocket. "No," Aron said, patting Lucius's shoulder. "No more going back. We end this now. Sam, you ready?"

"Yes."

The twins rose to their feet and locked hands. The beast wobbled forward and unleashed a furious roar. The wound from its stomach continued to leak a dark liquid; it flowed down its immense girth and created a puddle at its feet.

The twins didn't flinch. They stepped over Lucius and stood between him and the demon formally called Ms. Hemmings. Lucius watched in awe. This had never happened. They had never managed to inflict such damage, let alone have Aron survive this long.

Maybe this time would be different. Maybe this time they would finish the job.

The Battle of 1451 Turner Street

(Part II)

Mary Anne shoveled the unused flesh into a metal wastebasket sitting next to her table. She then tossed the bones onto an already existing pile by her furnace. She bundled up Agent Benjamin's suit and placed it neatly on top of the trash. The wastebasket screeched as she dragged it across the stone floor. The furnace's roaring fire beckoned for sustenance, and she was more than willing to oblige. She emptied the wastebasket into the inferno and watched the remains burn.

As much as she loathed humans, she did enjoy some of their activities. She had grown quite fond of cooking, in particular. She wasn't sure which aspect she enjoyed more: preparing the meal, watching the humans gleefully eat their own, or having them award her for it. Nonetheless, she hadn't felt this happy in centuries.

A toothy grin spread across her face as the IWPS stitching on Agent Benjamin's suit melted away. Justice had been served. The Invisible World Protective Service had imprisoned her for over four hundred years for a string of murders and kidnappings in the early 1500s. The original sentence had only been for two centuries, but they tacked on an additional two hundred years for the child remains they found later. She had no one but herself to blame. She had been young and inexperienced. After finally being released, she did abide by the rules of her parole for a couple of decades for fear of going back, but how long can you suppress who you truly are?

"A hawk is not persecuted for hunting mice…" Mary Anne mumbled. Her eyes continued to dance with the flames.

Her first few victims had reminded her of old times. The thrill of the kill was unrivaled. If she remembered correctly, the first three had been a paperboy, a trash man, and a traveling salesman. The process was simple enough: she lured them in and feasted. In order to properly feed, she had built a cellar. It provided her complete privacy, but a problem quickly arose. She rarely ate all that she killed—it was the hunt that satisfied her—and for a while, she was uncertain what to do with the surplus meat. It was this same problem that had led the IWPS to her doorstep centuries ago. She thought of just burning all of the extra meat, but she considered that too wasteful.

The solution came in the form of a flyer in the mail, an ad for the county fair inviting all willing participants to enter their annual chili contest. Mary Anne fancied herself quite the genius after she decided to use her leftovers as the meat for her chili. The unusable parts she decided to burn. Her system worked. She won thirteen county fair ribbons, and Benjamin would serve as the key ingredient to her fourteenth. IWPS agents checked in on her every year and never suspected a thing. Benjamin's visit, however, was the final straw. She was tired of hiding. She was tired of being monitored.

Rumor had it that a war was on the horizon, and if that was true, there was no longer a need to continue this charade. The IWPS would soon fall and receive their just desserts. She was only doing her part in fighting the good fight. It was then that Mary Anne heard her living room window open.

She smelled four individuals. The three children were unmistakable, but the other was something else. The fourth scent was neither human nor demon. It was an agent.

She smirked. "So they have come for me already? But why the children?"

Without another word, her human appearance began to melt away. Her head widened and her hair fell out. Her arms extended, scraping the floor, and her stomach expanded, falling past her knees. A large sack dropped from her chin and was engorged with a sticky acid. She was waddling toward the trapdoor when it suddenly sprang open and three small orbs dropped from above. She quickly swatted two of them against the wall where they exploded on contact. The third hit the side of her head and detonated. Mary Anne roared. It stung, but there was no serious damage done.

The agent was the next thing to come through. She wasn't fazed by the agent's teddy bear appearance. She had encountered far stranger things. She lunged forward. The agent was quick, just quick enough to avoid each of her blows, but still, he was nothing she couldn't handle. It was the children who dropped in after him that caught her by surprise. Two of the children, whose hands were interlocked, sent her soaring through the air with just a flick of the wrist.

"Fascinating. They're psychics. It's been awhile," she thought as she flew across the cellar.

Mary Anne crashed to the floor, and the agent dove on top of her stomach. Even though she managed to impale him with one of her claws, he was still able to pierce her gut with his sword.

"Ahhhhh!" she bellowed. Her intrigue had morphed into fear. She shot a stream of acid at the children, not so much to hit them but to distract them.

The children dove to the ground, and with their attention elsewhere, she quickly tossed the agent aside and bathed him in acid, regaining control of the situation. It was only her and the three children. They mumbled something amongst themselves before the two who shared a striking resemblance to one another—twins she assumed—stepped forward, hand in hand. They stood in front of the third one, who was still on the floor, as if to protect him.

Mary Anne snarled. Her stomach ached and continued to bleed, but she was still more than strong enough to handle *children*. Especially a couple of young psychics. She had dealt with far more experienced ones. The key was to not allow them time to concentrate. She stomped the ground viciously, causing the earth to shake violently. The floorboards overhead creaked and splintered, warning they might give way.

The children were too focused on remaining upright to brace for her attack. Mary Anne charged forward and her immense girth collided with the female child, propelling her through the air until she smacked into the wall behind them. The girl collapsed at the base of the wall, motionless.

Mary Anne picked the male up by his throat and slammed him to the ground. Crimson blood erupted from his mouth and splattered across his face. There would've been more if she hadn't tightened her grip around his throat. She provided him barely enough air to breathe, let alone cough.

"Enough!" a voice shouted from behind her. "You won't kill them again!"

Mary Anne looked up to see that the third child was now missing. She let go of the psychic and turned around to face the voice. She twisted around, but her injuries slowed her far more than she was willing to admit. The third child had taken a bone from her pile and broken it in half. He held a sharp piece in each hand. By the time she fully faced him, he had gathered enough momentum to shove both pieces of bone deep into her stomach. He savagely twisted them.

"AHHHHH!" she screamed.

"I've watched you kill them over and over...and did nothing but go back and try to fix it. I've seen enough!"

Mary Anne had no idea what he was talking about, nor did she have the time to decipher it. She was woozy. More and more blood gushed from her stomach. With the little strength she had left, she slashed at the child, catching him across his chest. He fell to the ground instantly. She wobbled backward, but soon her feet were no longer touching the ground. She was spun around against her will and faced the twins, both leaning against the wall, hand in hand. The boy held out his hand and slowly began to curl it into a fist. It dawned on Mary Anne that she may have gravely underestimated these children.

"Goodbye," the twins said in unison.

Mary Anne's head began to ache. She heard a loud snap between her ears as her skull cracked. Her eyes bulged from their sockets, far more than usual, as her head was crushed.

"No…" she managed to say just before her jaw snapped.

The last thing Mary Anne Hemmings saw was the boy's fist close.

1632 Turner Street:

Gary's Mess

The bedside table rocked against Gary's bed until he could no longer ignore it. He slammed his hand down on top of his phone, but to his surprise, it was not ringing. The steady vibration was coming from the table's drawer. Gary jolted upright. The phone that resided there only rang when there was a mess to be cleaned up. His hands quickly found the key taped to the drawer's underside, unlocked it, and grabbed hold of the phone.

"Hello," he answered.

"1451 Turner Street needs a wipe. The clock has stopped. You have four hours."

4 hours left

There was a click and nothing more. Gary returned the phone to the drawer it shared with a few of his other IWPS gadgets and jumped from his bed. Gary was a stocky man with prematurely gray hair, no doubt due to the stress induced by his job. He made a beeline to his closet and seized the IWPS-issued charcoal grey suit he saved for these occasions. From the corner of his closet, he grabbed a hose, which was attached to a large black container. He had been assigned to Turner Street only a month ago, and this was already his third wipe. Things had escalated far faster than the projections he had been given at the onset of his assignment. His gut told him something much bigger was brewing and the carnage at the last two sites did nothing to ease his nerves. In just the last month, he had cleaned up the remains of an agent at 1428 and an attack on a child at 1418.

Neither activity would have topped his list of favorite assignments, but in his line of work, no such list existed. Gary packed up his van and sped down Turner Street, taking full advantage of the lack of traffic during the *freeze*. It was about three in the morning, and the freeze would ensure it stayed that way for a few more hours. The freeze, an emergency protocol of the IWPS, was only used in order to clean up situations that might alert the human world to the existence of its invisible counterpart.

On his mad dash to the scene, the wings of an owl frozen in mid-flight caught his eye. The moonlight bounced off the wings at such an angle that, even at the speed Gary was traveling, he was forced to take note and marvel at its beauty. This was his favorite part of his job, the calm that the freeze provided. When a freeze was in effect, anything that was neither an agent nor demon was frozen in place for the duration of the freeze. The only exceptions were humans who were issued specially de-signed IWPS wristbands that negated the freeze's effect. Most of these humans were survivors of the event that required the freeze, but very few of those humans existed.

3 hours left

At last, Gary's car pulled up to 1451 Turner Street. It was a circus. Neatly dressed men and women of all shapes and sizes combed the scene. Before Gary reached to open his door, he shook his right hand to feel the weight of his wristband. It was a nervous habit he had developed over the years.

"Just another mess, Gary, that's it," he whispered to himself.

Knock…Knock…Knock

A large man stood beside Gary's door. His meaty knuckles left sweaty prints on the window. Gary wound down his window.

"Yes, sir?"

"There's one agent and one demon down, plus three human survivors with varying degrees of injury, all of which could possibly need memory adjustments."

"Possible recruits?"

"Possible. But that's a matter for later. We only have three hours left, and you have your work cut out for you."

"Yes, Captain."

The captain walked away and was lost in the sea of suits. Gary gathered his tools and followed. He jostled his way through the crowd, clumsily dodging bodies with every step. He was in awe of the urgency at which the agents moved. Each step and gesture seemed to have a distinct purpose. No amount of energy went to waste.

"I need the cleaner now!" a tall thin man yelled from the front doorstep. Gary was spit from the sea of bodies and stood before him. "Sir?"

"I need a full cleaning of the house and demolition of the cellar. All clothes, dishes, and every piece of evidence of Ms. Hemmings's existence have already been removed from the residence. Finish the rest."

Gary nodded, brushed past the thin man, and went into the house.

2 hours left

Gary stood alone in the cellar in silence. The remains of Ms. Hemmings's head decorated the walls, floor, and ceiling. The rest of her body was a crumpled heap in the middle of the room.

"Must've been one hell of a fight…" he muttered.

He opened his black container and poured a dark green liquid in. He aimed the hose at the body and sprayed. The corpse began to melt the instant the liquid made contact. He then turned the hose to the wall and ceiling, respectively. It wasn't long before an inch-deep of liquid goo covered the floor. Just as quickly as the goo had puddled up, it began to evaporate. Thirty minutes later, Gary stood in a spotless cellar. He then pulled out four circular charges from his pockets and stuck them to each wall. Finally, he climbed the ladder out of the cellar and detonated the charges.

In each of the remaining rooms of the house, Gary placed what he affectionately referred to as the "AXE can." The container's striking resemblance to the famous body spray and his habit of regularly spraying too much made the comparison easy. Sadly, the agents weren't high on humor, and the joke was usually met with blank stares and head shaking.

Once each can was in place, he cleared the house and initiated the final part of the cleaning. Upon activation, the cans let loose a spray that vaporized all traces of agent, human, and demon fingerprints and odors.

1 hour left

Gary left the house and grabbed the first agent walking by.

"Where are the humans who survived?"

The agent pointed to the edge of the lawn where three

children sat, each sporting an IWPS bracelet. The freeze was almost over, and the sea of agents had thinned. It didn't take long before Gary reached the children and tapped the biggest on his shoulder. He had a strange birthmark on his neck.

"Are you three okay?"

The boy lightly tapped his chest and winced. "Yeah, I guess. I'm Lucius, and that's Aron and Samantha."

"It's nice to meet you all. There's no reason to beat around the bush. I understand exactly what you guys have been through." Gary showed them his bracelet. "And believe me, if the agency offers you a job, take it. You don't want to have your memories erased. If you guys are capable of doing what I saw in that cellar again, then the war may not be so one-sided after all."

"War..." Samantha said solemnly.

"One-sided?" Aron asked.

"Yeah. The agency won't admit it, but a war is coming. And even by the most conservative estimates, we are greatly outmatched. The demons have become more aggressive and have steadily whittled down our numbers."

The children just stared. "There hasn't been a demon

incident of this magnitude since…well, me, ten years ago," Gary said. "There have been two other incidents of lesser degree this month on Turner Street *alone*. Something is coming and it's coming here."

"What can we do?" Samantha asked.

"Be the difference," the captain said from behind Gary. "We aim to protect children above all else. However, when *anomalies*, children with special abilities, are trained properly, they can be our best counter to the demon threat. But we only recruit those who have experienced the problem firsthand. Will you help us?"

No one answered. "How will you guys explain Ms. Hemmings's disappearance to her neighbors?" Aron finally asked.

"All evidence of her stay at this house has been thoroughly removed. All that's left is to put a For Sale sign up. People move all the time. And we'll handle the neighbors who don't buy that story. Unfortunately, we'll be forced to tamper with their minds, like yours, if you decide not to help us."

"We'll help," Aron said.

"Excellent," the captain continued. "But first, we require the assistance of one more anomaly from Turner Street and we'll need your help to get him."

0 hours left

1654 Turner Street:

Jamie & Titus

Jamie emerged from his closet and into his room. His eyes were focused solely on his bed, which sat directly in front of him. Nothing else mattered. He started toward it but stumbled. His legs could no longer support him. Each step was an arduous task. His arms were lead pipes by his side, and the weight of his eyelids had become more than he could bear. As he collapsed to the floor, he was caught by something sturdy and covered in fur. His body landed on the head of a large lion that had been following closely behind him. The massive beast nearly filled Jamie's small room, and its rear was still inside the closet. The lion used its head to flip Jamie onto its back and carried him to his bed. It then shrugged its shoulders, launching Jamie into the air. He landed peacefully on top of his mattress. Finally, the lion squeezed the rest of its body into the room and rested its head on Jamie's chest.

"Attaboy," Jamie mumbled.

He scratched behind his best friend's ears and patted his head. With each stroke, Jamie felt more of his strength and energy returning. A few minutes passed before Jamie opened his eyes again. When he did, a lion cub no bigger than his forearm was curled up on his chest.

"Titus?" Jamie whispered. The cub purred and wiggled.

Jamie used his pillows to prop himself up, and Titus slid down into his lap, still sleeping. Jamie stared at the sleeping cub and an overwhelming sense of security fell over him. Since Titus had arrived a few years ago, he had rarely felt otherwise. However, Titus's origin was still a mystery to him. One night, he just showed up.

***

Titus first appeared a couple of nights before Jamie's seventh birthday. On the night of his arrival, Jamie had again overheard his parents arguing about their favorite topic of discussion: him.

"You can't expect him to watch those movies and not have nightmares, John!" Jamie's mother roared.

"When I was a kid, I used to watch those same kinds of movies with my dad all the time," Jamie's father answered. "Sure, I had a few nightmares here and there, but I turned out just fine. I don't see what the big deal is…"

"The big deal…the *big deal* is that your son can't go to sleep because he swears he's hearing monsters in his closet. I think that's a big deal!"

"Lay off it, Mary, the kid will be alright."

"And that's your problem, John…"

Jamie closed his bedroom door and sulked on the floor. His latest attempt to convince his parents of the monsters in his closet had failed. Their response to his cries for help was their usual closet inspection. They turned on the light, peered in, and moved a few clothes around. They again found nothing and shut the door. However, unbeknownst to them, the bloodcurdling cries of the ravenous beasts hidden in the darkness returned the instant the closet door shut. While they reminded Jamie of the moral behind the story of *The Boy Who Cried Wolf* and lectured him on the nonexistence of monsters, a chorus of hungry beasts played as background music. It wasn't long after his parents left his room that their current argument had begun.

Jamie pulled his knees to his chest and rocked back and forth to the terrifying sounds coming from his closet. He tried to focus his mind on anything other than the howling, and his mind settled on a documentary he had recently watched with his father. It followed a lion pride and their leader, Titus.

"If Titus was here, he'd protect me," he whispered.

Jamie suddenly heard a soft purr from under his bed. The color immediately drained from his face. He had never heard anything from under there before. His fear paralyzed him. His eyes were fixed on the darkness under his bed as he waited for whatever it was to devour him. Suddenly, two yellow eyes appeared in the darkness. They locked with Jamie's, and astonishingly, his fear promptly dissipated. Those eyes carried no malice or hatred, only love. A lion cub wobbled from under his bed and sat in front of him. The roars from Jamie's closet intensified, but Jamie was not fazed.

"Titus?" Jamie asked.

The cub squeaked as it tried to roar and then slowly began to grow. Before Jamie's eyes, Titus rapidly aged into adulthood. His shoulders widened and his back lengthened. His tail thickened and landed on the floor with a *thud.* Muscle wrapped around his four legs and bulged underneath his fur. At last, a golden mane erupted from his neck and framed his face. Titus turned to the closet and unleashed a primal roar that must have radiated from the very pit of his stomach. Just like the ones Jamie had heard on TV. The roar swallowed up the bloodthirsty cries from the closet, and all was silent.

Titus faced Jamie. He was ten times the size he had been as a cub, but the love in his eyes remained the same. Jamie smiled but felt unusually tired. All his energy had abruptly vanished, and he could hardly sit upright. As he fell to one side, Titus lounged forward and Jamie landed in his mane. It was soft and smelled of fresh strawberries, his favorite dessert. Jamie buried his face in it and stroked it gently. As he continued to rub against it, his strength slowly returned. Within moments, Titus was again a cub and sleeping at his feet.

His parents were not the least bit thrilled the next

morning when he explained to them he had a pet lion. Just like the monsters in his closet, Titus was invisible to them. According to his parents, Titus was a figment of his imagination.

***

Repeated knocks on the doorframe of his closet brought Jamie back to the present. His head whipped toward it. In the doorway was Captain Lewis of the Invisible World Protective Service, accompanied by three children—two of which, a boy and girl, were nearly identical.

"May we enter?" the captain asked.

"If you must," Jamie answered. "I thought only demons used closets?"

Jamie patted Titus, who stood alert on his bed. He had grown to the size of an adolescent lion.

Captain Lewis strolled through the doorway. "These are desperate times, Jamie, rules change."

Titus snarled. "Easy, boy," Jamie whispered.

"I see you have better control of Titus now. If this had been anything like the last time I saw you two, he would've been fully grown and on top of us before I even knocked."

"We've been together a long time now," Jamie answered. "Why are you here?"

"I need your help, Jamie."

Jamie ignored the plea and pointed to the kids. "Who are they?"

"Anomalies," the captain answered.

"We're going to help you," the girl said. "I'm Samantha, and this is my twin brother, Aron." She tugged the arm of the boy with whom she shared a striking resemblance.

"My name is Lucius," the tallest and apparent oldest said, raising his hand.

"This is your team for the mission ahead," the captain said.

"No." Jamie got off his bed, and Titus followed. He had now reached early adulthood.

"We don't have time for this, Jamie. And speaking of time you're getting pretty old now. What are you now? Fourteen? Fifteen?"

"It doesn't matter."

"Thirteen and a half," Aron answered pointing to his head. "Your mind is an open book, man."

Titus, now fully grown, let loose a roar that caused

the intruders to immediately retreat closer to the closet door.

"Stay out of my head!" Jamie sneered. "I don't need some brainwashed kid stumbling around in there."

"What do you mean, brainwashed?" Aron shot back.

Jamie chuckled. "Did you tell them what happens if they don't help the IWPS when asked, Captain?"

The captain was silent. "What happens?" Aron demanded. The captain still said nothing.

"If you don't work for them, they'll '*neutralize*' you on your eighteenth birthday. When you're no longer a kid," Jamie answered.

Titus snarled and glared at the captain.

"Neutralize?" Samantha asked.

"Once you have passed the age threshold and entered adulthood, you are far more susceptible to the temptation of demons," the captain explained. "It is no longer about feeding. It's about taking possession of you and your abilities. The IWPS can't risk that."

"I thought adults couldn't see demons?" Samantha asked.

"No," the captain answered. "It just takes much more

effort to get their attention, and adult anomalies are worth the effort."

"So you would kill us?" Lucius hissed. "When were you going to tell us this?"

The captain's expression was stern and unwavering. "You would have been informed no sooner or later than when you expressed the desire to leave the IWPS."

"You're no different than the demons," Jamie sneered.

"We give you a choice," the captain answered. "You four make up a very small percentage of the children in the world. However, the side that possesses your gifts will hold the upper hand. I do not take this decision lightly. The protection of all children is my sole purpose, but once you have crossed that threshold, you are no longer under my jurisdiction. And I must neutralize all threats to my purpose."

Titus roared again, but this time he took a step forward. The children took a step back, but the captain held his ground.

"We don't work for you!" Jamie shouted.

"This is about more than you and me, Jamie. I understand it is difficult to see that now, and I am sorry that I must put such a weight on your shoulders. But I have a duty to all the children of this world."

"I have done more in the last few nights than your entire organization has done in months."

"Your accomplishments have been well documented, but if you do not join this team, I will be forced to return in five years to neutralize both you and Titus. On that day, there will be no conversation. If I am forced to return, my job will be my only concern."

Titus stepped back toward Jamie and quickly began to shrink. Samantha then stepped forward. "We're in this together, Jamie. We're a team now."

"You're not the only one who wants to see nineteen. Plus, we could use a lion on the team," Aron added.

"And working for the IWPS sounds better than both possession and execution," Lucius chimed in.

Jamie shook his head and picked up Titus. "I don't have much of a choice now, do I? I'm in."

1431 Turner Street:

Lucius's Future

Lucius sat in his kitchen alone and in complete darkness. Since the incident at Ms. Hemmings's house, he had been hesitant to use his time machine, and of course his current orders demanded he do just that. His stomach ached and his head was light. He hadn't eaten in days. The burden of knowing what may lie ahead in the future was a burden he no longer wished to bear. After countless jumps, his last effort to alter the future had finally worked out. He had managed to save the twins, but it came at a great cost.

Each alternate timeline was just as real to him as the one in which he was currently living. While he slept, every memory replayed in his head like a sadistic gag reel.

He had relived Aron's death so many times and in so many variations that the fact Aron was now alive seemed *wrong*. Understandably, the twins were grateful for his intervention, but that didn't erase the memories. Lucius had cradled Aron's lifeless body. His blood had drenched Lucius's clothing. But these details were deemed necessary evils by the IWPS. His orders were to ignore the memories and focus only on *this* reality. Easier said than done.

The idea that their war against the demons was bigger than any single individual had been drilled into the mind of each member of the team. Everybody had a role to play, and Lucius's was to help them avoid any potential pitfalls by scouting the future and providing "do-overs" when necessary.

"But at what cost?" Lucius mumbled.

Lucius reached for his time machine, which could best be described as a calculator. He quickly entered his intended date, but his hand hovered over the circular red button that read "Enter."

Who knows what could be waiting for me? Lucius thought.

He sighed. "But there's only one way to find out."

His index finger pressed Enter and a blue light on the corner of the device began to flash repeatedly. He was immediately encapsulated in an opaque blue sphere. Within seconds, the sphere was gone and he stood in the middle of what used to be his kitchen. His house was no more; only its ruins remained. The kitchen was filled with charred debris, and the walls that still stood looked more like Swiss cheese than the foundations of a home. The roof had been destroyed, allowing him an excellent view of the ruby-red sky above and the branches of an unnaturally enormous tree.

"What happened here…" he mumbled.

Lucius waded through the ashes that covered the floor of his home. He was able to squeeze through one of the larger holes in the outer walls of his house and into the outside world. Turner Street was a disaster. The neatly kept homes that had lined the street in his time had either been entirely destroyed or only their foundations remained. The road had been replaced by scorched earth.

"You're right on time," said a voice to his right.

Lucius turned to see a one-armed man. His black hair was long and unkempt. Clumps of dirt were clearly visible in his locks. He offered a weary smile that Lucius found even more unsettling than the destruction that was before him.

"Aron?"

"Yeah." His smile faded. "It's a pretty bleak future, huh?"

Lucius surveyed his surroundings once more. "What happened?"

Aron shrugged. "We lost…it wasn't even close."

"You don't seem too shaken up about it."

"The war ended twenty years ago. The others died five years after that, and they got you last week. I don't have any more grief left to give."

"But how did it happen?"

As Aron walked closer and closed the gap between them, his nonchalant demeanor melted away. He stood inches from Lucius, deathly serious.

"You are planning to change this, right?"

Lucius hesitated. "What?"

Aron tapped his temple with his remaining arm. "I'm a little bit stronger than when I was twelve, those mental blocks won't hold me anymore. Your mind is nearly wide open, but you have managed to keep your reasoning hidden from me…Lucius, how could you not want to avoid this?" Aron asked, flabbergasted.

"Get out of my head!" Lucius screamed.

"Not until you give me an answer!" Aron shouted. "I buried my sister. I lost my arm. I need to know why you don't want to prevent this."

Lucius shook his head. "I can't keep doing this…I never forget…None of the memories go away."

Aron squeezed Lucius's shoulder. "Lucius, you have to keep jumping until you get it right. We were able to change things once, weren't we? We can do it again."

"I don't know…"

Aron smiled. "You know, a few weeks ago you told me that we would meet here. You said that I would have to be pretty convincing in order to get your head out of your butt."

Lucius chuckled, and soon they were both laughing, but it was short-lived.

"How did they get me?" Lucius asked hesitantly.

"An ambush. You saved my life."

"And the others?"

"We lost Jamie and Titus during our raid of the demon stronghold after the IWPS fell. They got Sam when…" Aron trailed off. His eyes glistened, and he quickly turned his head. "They got her and my arm at the same time…"

"I'm sorry," Lucius whispered. That was all he could say. Lucius wouldn't pretend to understand the gravity of Aron's loss. Aron and Samantha were inseparable. Individually, the twins had the gift of telepathy, but their telekinesis was only generated when they made contact with one another. The majority of the time, they held hands. To have lost so much at once was inconceivable.

Aron wiped his eyes. "I don't need your sympathy. I need your help."

"I can't…"

"Look around you, Lucius!" Aron interrupted. "Everyone is gone. They killed and ate *everyone*. My group has twenty survivors left, at most. Our numbers shrink every day. You are our only hope."

"But if your timeline's version of me already made this trip and knew I would come, how did this still happen?

And why didn't he just keep jumping back to save you?"

"Because, when he jumped here, I wasn't here to meet him. He hadn't told me to do so yet. So we had to live through all of this in order to get the message to you. Plus, his time machine was destroyed shortly after the war began. Meaning in this timeline, you lost your ability to jump."

Lucius shook his head. "Jumping never gets any simpler. I just don't know if I can keep doing this, Aron."

Aron sighed. "We were all kids back then, you know. We all saw things reserved for our worst nightmares, but we fought on because it was the right thing to do. Sam was right. If we have the power to do something, then we have the responsibility to do so. If we don't, then this future is guaranteed for you, as well."

Lucius said nothing. "I know the memories are bad," Aron continued. "But we all made tremendous sacrifices. And this is one you have to make in order to save us all." He stretched his arm wide. "All of us."

Lucius sighed. "What do you need me to do?"

Aron nodded. "You see that tree?"

Lucius nodded. "Yeah, where did that thing come

from? It's huge."

"We don't know, but our best bet is to ask Jamie. He knows the IWPS inside and out. But he had already died by the time we knew what to ask him."

"Ask him what?"

"About Witness 942."

"Who?"

"Exactly. That's what you have to find out. We tried to figure it out without him, but the IWPS was long gone by the time we learned about the witness. We pried it out of a demon we captured and tortured. All we know for sure is that Witness 942 was last seen during the months leading up to the war. He is directly related to that tree. That tree somehow endowed the demon armies with more than enough power to topple us. If you can stop that tree from sprouting, you can save your timeline."

"What does Jamie have to do with any of this?"

"Witness 942 was under IWPS custody. Jamie was involved with the IWPS in various degrees for years before us. He was one of their best assets. If anyone knows, it's him."

"I'll do my best." Lucius began to dial a date into his time machine.

Aron wrapped his arm around Lucius. "I didn't get a chance to tell you, thanks for saving me, again."

Aron let go, and Lucius pressed Enter.

1632 Turner Street:

Charles's Tree

Charles took a sip of coffee. The rich flavor spread across his palate, and he was reminded that there were things he adored about the human world. He settled into his seat under a green umbrella at a coffee shop at the end of Turner Street. He hadn't expected to make another appearance this early in the proceedings, but this particular situation needed his personal attention. The recent intel Charles had received concerning Gary Laneburg's survival had thrown a rather large wrench into his plan. The name had not crossed his mind in nearly a decade, and for good reason. At the time, he had been assured by his lieutenants that the child had been killed. However, according to his mole in the Invisible World Protective Service, this was not the case.

Gary was alive and well. In fact, he was even an IWPS employee. To be more precise, he was a cleaner for the IWPS's infamous freeze operations. It wasn't that this human's survival scared Charles; it was that he represented an unnecessary loose end that needed to be tied up. He took another sip of coffee, sighed, and poured some more cream into his cup. Competent help was hard to come by these days. The IWPS had labeled Gary as "Witness 942," and he was the only person who knew exactly what Charles had dug up from Gary's backyard on that fateful night all those years ago. It was time to find out who else he told.

Charles flipped his empty cup into the nearby trash bin and began to walk down Turner Street. A Missing Dog poster for a St. Bernard caught his eye, and he smiled. It was the tenth one he had seen that day. His sunglasses gleamed in the dying rays of sunshine. His sleek black suit clung tightly to his body. His stride was long but slow. He moved purposefully but was in no hurry. His job would be completed regardless of when he arrived. The sun had nearly set in the distance, and its failing light created long shadows as its claim to the day was relinquished.

On his journey, Charles approached a group of very young children playing in the front yard of 1789 Turner Street. They immediately fell silent. Charles's unusually pointy ears twitched, and he smirked while he listened to their racing hearts. He turned his head and waved as he passed by. He lifted his sunglasses, and his smile widened to a wicked grin.

"It's the boogeyman!" the children shrieked and sprinted inside.

Charles lowered his glasses and laughed. It was the little things that brought him the most joy. The last bit of sunlight faded, and the shadows took hold of the land. It wouldn't be much longer until he arrived. He left the sidewalk and trotted up the driveway of 1632 Turner Street. He whistled a wistful melody, no song in partic-ular but a hodgepodge of somber tunes. At last, he knocked on the door and waited. It wasn't long before a stout young man answered. He took one look at Charles and dropped the glass of clear liquid he was holding. His mouth hung open. Charles removed his glasses. There was nothing there but empty black holes. He smiled a horrific smile and revealed rows of pointy teeth.

"Hello, Gary. Or is it Witness 942?"

"I…"

But Gary couldn't finish. Charles's arm shot out, and his long fingers wrapped tightly around Gary's throat. He lifted Gary off his feet and forced his way into his home. Charles slammed Gary's head into a wall, and plaster sprayed in all directions.

"Gary, do you know why I'm here?"

Gary wheezed and gasped. Charles relaxed his grip only slightly so that Gary could breathe.

"Because…I…saw…the seed…" Gary spat out.

"Yes, Gary, and who did you tell?" Charles continued to ease his grip.

"No one, I swear. I only told the IWPS that I saw you. Nothing more."

"I don't believe you." Charles tightened his grip and bashed Gary's head repeatedly into the wall. When Charles had finally stopped, Gary was a mess. One of Gary's eyes was swollen shut. The right side of his head bled profusely. Charles loosened his grip again, and Gary spit out four teeth.

"Who did you tell?"

Gary coughed up blood. "No one…AHHHHH!"

Before Gary finished, Charles grabbed his left arm and in one fluid motion peeled it off his body like string cheese. He tossed it over his shoulder and it landed by the door.

"You know, Gary, I believed you all along." Charles laughed. "I just didn't appreciate the fact that I had to come all this way to handle something that should've been taken care of a decade ago."

Gary mumbled something, and to Charles's astonishment, Gary smiled.

"What's so funny?"

"You…you won't win."

"Oh, I thought you actually had something meaningful to say." Charles dropped Gary to the floor. He then reached into his front pocket and pulled out a small seed. Charles squatted down so that he was at Gary's eye level.

"This is what you saw me dig up that night." Charles shook the seed in the palm of his hand. "Honestly, you just happened to be at the wrong place at the wrong time. So were your parents." Charles shrieked with laughter.

"They…will…k-k-kill you," Gary stuttered.

"Shhh, Gary, I wasn't finished. This isn't just any seed, you see. It's the Cain Seed. It's one of a kind. It took me a very long time to track it down. Within its shell is *every* wicked deed that mankind has ever committed, and from it will sprout the Tree of Death. Its power will galvanize and fuel my armies. I buried the seed in what would become your backyard centuries before you were born. Unfortunately for you, when I came to collect it, your family was living there."

Gary's head bobbed up and down. His eyes rolled to the back of his head, revealing only the whites as his body went into shock. Charles dug two fingers into the shoulder of Gary's missing arm.

"Ahhhhh!" Gary cried. Tears rolled down his grimy cheeks.

"Don't fall asleep on me, Gary." Charles licked his fingers. "You're probably wondering why I haven't killed you yet, huh?"

Gary said nothing. Charles grabbed Gary's head and nodded it for him.

"I knew you were curious. Now, as I was saying, the Cain Seed is unlike any other seed. It doesn't require soil to grow but flesh; human flesh." Charles smiled. "You see, I learned it requires a host, Gary. Meaning I'm nowhere near finished with you. You will be the nourishment for my tree. The Tree of Death will sprout from your body. Your blood will feed its roots, and when its first flower blooms, I will lead my legions against the humans. Humanity's own sins will be their ultimate undoing. Poetic, right?"

Gary moaned. Charles chuckled and then plunged the seed deep into the bloody hole that used to be Gary's arm.

"It's now just a matter of time," Charles said. "Anyway, we should be on our way, Gary. You and I will be the best of pals until the sprouting. But before we go, there's one more thing."

Charles stuck his fingers into Gary's mouth and ripped out his tongue. "I don't want you spilling any of my secrets on the off-chance I lose you."

"Get away from him!" a voice from behind Charles shouted.

Charles peeked over his shoulder. Standing just inside the door were four children, one of whom sat atop a lion. Another one, taller than the rest with a strange mark on his neck, held what looked like a calculator in his hand. The last two children, a boy and girl who shared a strong resemblance, were holding hands.

"What is this supposed to be?" Charles sneered.

"Get away from him, demon!" the child atop the lion yelled again.

"I don't have time for this." Charles rose to his feet and grabbed Gary's remaining arm.

"You're not going anywhere," the female child said.

Charles let go of Gary's arm. "I suppose I could use a snack before I leave."

The boy, who was holding hands with the girl, lifted his free arm and beckoned at Gary's body. To Charles's amazement, Gary's body rose into the air and drifted toward the children by the door.

"It won't be that easy." Charles snatched Gary's body and threw it back to the ground. He pressed his foot against Gary's chest, pinning him down. Charles grinned. "But at least this will be interesting. Please don't disappoint me."

1632 Turner Street:
The Brody Twins II

Samantha stood in the foyer of Gary's house with her twin brother Aron, the time traveler Lucius, and their de facto leader Jamie and his pet lion, Titus. It was a motley crew, to say the least, but together they formed Gary's sole chance of survival. Samantha was unable to shake the gnawing guilt that she was responsible for her and Aron's current predicament. It was she, after all, who had guilt-tripped him into investigating Ms. Hemmings's house. It was she who had continued to volunteer them for missions, and now they were so deep in the rabbit hole that they could only dream of crawling out.

According to Jamie, who due to his vigilante activity had the most field experience, they were now moments away from going toe-to-toe with one of the most noto-rious demons the IWPS had ever encountered. The de-mon across from them, known only as Charles, was a tall, slender humanoid dressed in a black suit. However, one look at its face quickly erased any notion that it could be human at all.

The demon's eyes were gaping black holes. Saliva dripped in long, stringy strands from its open mouth, which contained rows of short, sharp teeth. In one of its arms it held Gary's mangled body. His face resembled a Picasso painting. He was not in good shape. Samantha's eyes were drawn to the wide bleeding hole where his arm used to be. Her hands were clammy, and her grip on her brother's hand tightened. They again faced the very real possibility of dying.

Unlike their battle with Ms. Hemmings, there was no agent Jericho to help them, and there was no backup coming from the IWPS. Lucius and Jamie had been con-vinced that they needed to go to Gary's immediately. Lucius's last trip to the future fueled this belief. There had been no time to contact the IWPS, and from the looks of things, they'd made the right decision.

Gary had once told Lucius, Aron, and Samantha that they were the key to winning this war, and Samantha desperately hoped he was right. According to the future that Lucius described, if they didn't save Gary now, they would sentence the entire human race to extinction.

"I'm sorry," Samantha said telepathically to Aron.

"Don't be, it's our duty, remember? Let's save Gary," Aron responded.

Aron stretched out his hand and beckoned at Gary's limp body. Gary rose and slowly began to approach the children.

"It won't be that easy," Charles sneered. It ripped Gary from the air and threw him to the floor. The demon planted its foot onto Gary's chest. The corners of the demon's mouth turned upright into a hellish smile.

"But at least this will be interesting. Please don't disappoint me."

The demon's coat sleeves suddenly stretched down past his hands and hit the floor. His arms had formed into two long spears.

"Watch out for those!" Jamie shouted.

In the time it took Samantha to blink, one of Charles's

arms shot out toward her and Aron. Aron quickly waved his hand across his body, causing Charles's arm to rocket off course and into the closet to the right of them. Charles's arm retracted, leaving a large hole in the door and giving a clear view into a coat closet.

"Those spear things are his arms!" Jamie shouted. "They can stretch, bend, and turn any way he sees fit. Stay on your toes! Titus, let's go!"

The massive lion let loose a ferocious roar that forced Charles off balance. Jamie and Titus took advantage of the moment and raced forward. Charles's arms shot at the duo in every which way, but they evaded every blow.

"We need to help them!" Lucius shouted.

"Stay back, Lucius, we need you alive just in case we need a do-over. We will handle this." Aron squeezed his sister's hand.

"Jamie and Titus know what they're doing. They have more experience than all of us," Samantha said. "We'll cover them, and when the opportunity presents itself, you get Gary."

"Okay," Lucius answered.

Jamie and Titus were nearing Charles but appeared to

have made a misstep as one of Charles's arms knocked them off balance. Before Charles's other arm could deliver a finishing blow, the twins raised their free hands and aimed them at the stumbling duo. The twins coated Jamie and Titus in a transparent force field just in time to protect them from a devastating hit. The arm ricocheted off the force field and through the ceiling. Titus balanced himself and barreled into Charles's chest. The force of the hit sent the three of them crashing deeper into Gary's house, leaving Gary sprawled on the floor.

"Lucius, get Gary!" The twins ran after Jamie and Titus with their arms extended.

The twins found them in the kitchen. Titus was on top of Charles with one of Charles's arms between his jaws. Titus's head thrashed wildly side to side as he tried to tear it off. In the meantime, Charles's free arm bashed madly against the force field.

"Ahhhhh! Let go of my arm, you wretched beast!" Charles screamed. His attacks on the force field became increasingly more vicious. The twins further exerted themselves in order to maintain the force field, and

Samantha began to feel lightheaded. Her strength in her arm waned.

"Sam, stay with me, they need us," Aron pleaded.

Charles's attention suddenly turned to the twins. His free arm rocketed at Samantha. Samantha tried to move, but her legs were heavy and she barely had enough energy to stand. Aron released her hand and shoved her to the ground. Charles's arm missed her but then immediately curved back toward Jamie and Titus. Without physical contact, the twins could no longer access their telekinetic abilities and produce the force field. As a result, Charles's arm torpedoed through Jamie's chest.

Jamie let loose a blood-chilling scream. In response, Titus gave one last vicious tug on Charles's arm and ripped it clean off.

"AHHHHH!" Charles shrieked. His remaining arm retreated from Jamie's chest. Titus stumbled backward and collapsed to the floor. Jamie was motionless beside him.

"No…" Samantha whispered.

"He'll be okay, Sam, look." Aron pointed at Titus. The lion was quickly shrinking, and as he shrank, the pool of blood around Jamie stopped spreading. When Titus was again a cub, Jamie scooped him up and slowly rose to his feet. The hole in his chest was no more.

"Now you have to get up, Sam," Aron hissed.

With Aron's help, Samantha wobbled to her feet. Charles, too, was standing. His shoulder was leaking a black liquid.

"You have accomplished nothing!" he screamed. "I will kill you all!"

"Not before we take your other arm." Lucius walked up next to the twins.

"Lucius, where's Gary?" Samantha asked.

"He's safe, and he gave me this." Lucius held up a remote with a single red button.

"What's that?" Charles hissed.

"The cavalry," Lucius responded. "An IWPS distress beacon. Gary had it in his dresser. I pushed it five minutes ago."

Right on cue, the coat closet door in the foyer burst open and a sea of IWPS agents flooded the house.

"No!" Charles's remaining arm whipped toward the twins and Lucius, but he was tackled by agents before it was able to reach them. The agents quickly stabbed Charles with a syringe filled with a blue liquid. Charles was instantly still.

"The freeze begins now." Captain Lewis entered the house from the closet. "Get that demon out of here."

Jamie cradled Titus in his arms and joined the rest of the team. "I guess we did okay, huh?"

They answered with matching weary smiles.

"Will Titus be alright?" Samantha asked.

"He'll probably be out for the next week or two. He had to give me all his energy in order to heal my chest, but yeah, he'll be okay."

From behind them, someone cleared their throat and they all jumped. It was the captain. "This was foolish, and you should've been killed. But clearly you weren't, and because of you we now have Charles. For that, I thank you. Next time, just tell me so I can provide backup. You are still children."

"What about Gary?" Lucius asked.

"Gary is no longer your concern." The captain turned and disappeared into the crowd of agents.

"Can you believe that guy?"

"Forget him, Lucius, we do *work* for him. He doesn't have to tell us anything," Aron said.

"So, what do we do now?" Samantha asked.

"Get some sleep," Jamie answered.

They all laughed, and for a moment they actually resembled children.

TURN THE PAGE FOR A
SNEAK PEAK AT THE NEXT
BOOK IN THE TURNER
STREET CHRONICLES

The Cain Seed

Turner Street Chronicles Book II

1735 Turner Street:
Billy's Tale

With winter came peace on Turner Street. A blanket of white powder covered the perfectly manicured lawns, and the brisk December breeze swept away the multitude of sins that had polluted the air just months ago. During this time of peace, Billy found a new lease on life. With his overbearing parents out of town and his aunt from the neighboring county babysitting for a couple of weeks, Billy had a lot to look forward to. His aunt was far more hands-off than his mother. When she visited, all restrictions were lifted. Billy was now free to explore the winter wonderland that was his front yard.

Months had passed since his parents last allowed him to play outside, and Billy was tired of being caged in his room. He was not a dog. But even though he hated to admit it, his parents had reason to be protective. He was only ten, after all, and Turner Street had recently fallen victim to a rash of strange occurrences. A few of his friends from around the block had even gone missing—and had never turned up. It was a scary time. However, since last week, that no longer bothered him. All of that felt like a lifetime ago.

Things seemed different now; he was different now. He had finally gotten over the *incident* from last week. His parents, on the other hand, were unable to let it go. They rarely acknowledged him now. To add further insult to injury, he awoke this morning and they had gone on vacation without him. But things weren't all bad. He did get to enjoy this great day outside.

Billy put on the thickest jacket he owned and his warmest hat. He did not want to catch a cold. His mother would never let him hear the end of it. The snow in his front yard was up to his shins. Even his aunt's SUV in the driveway was completely covered. To Billy's delight, the snow was the perfect consistency for making a snowman, and that was exactly how he was going to spend his day. He picked up a clump of snow and slowly molded it into a sphere. He then placed it on the ground and rolled it until it was large enough to provide his snowman with a sturdy base.

He labored for hours, and at last a tidy snowman stood before him. He took a carrot from the fridge for the nose, used raisins to outline the mouth, and topped it off with his father's favorite bucket hat.

Billy took a step back and admired his work. From the corner of his eye he saw the outline of someone standing on the sidewalk, watching him. Without flinching, he turned to face the stranger. He felt no fear at all. He found this particularly surprising, since under no circumstance would he ever consider himself brave. He rarely slept without his nightlight or without checking his closet twice before crawling into bed. The only time he could remember not following this nightly routine was right before *it* happened. He would never do that again.

As it turned out, the stranger wasn't a stranger at all. It was Amelia from down the street. He was pretty sure she lived at 1428. Her long, brown hair rested on her shoulders and perfectly framed her round face. Her brown eyes were a few shades darker than her caramel skin. She smiled and ran over to Billy.

Billy's own smile spread from ear to ear. "Amelia! Where have you been?"

Her smile shrank slightly. "I've been around."

"Everyone's been looking for you. Your parents came over yesterday and talked with mine for a while. Everyone was crying." Billy paused. "But I bet they were really surprised when you came back, huh?"

Amelia's smile vanished. "I don't think I'm allowed to go back, Billy."

"Why not?"

"It's just not how it works." Amelia shook her head. "I thought you knew that already."

"What are you talking about?"

"Never mind," she sighed. "Anyway, I saw your snowman, can I check it out?"

"Yeah, sure," Billy said.

Amelia turned and pored over Billy's creation. While she was poking the snowman's carrot nose, Billy noticed that she was not wearing a coat. She was actually in her pajamas, a yellow onesie.

"Aren't you cold?" Billy asked.

"No, I'm okay." Amelia took a raisin from the snowman's mouth and popped it into her own.

"Hey," Billy sighed. "I worked hard on that."

"Still...nothing," Amelia muttered.

Billy grabbed Amelia's shoulder and spun her around. "What's wrong with you?"

"I didn't want this, Billy. I didn't want to go!"

"What?" Billy scratched his head.

"I didn't want to go!" she screamed.

"I'm going to get my aunt," Billy said and ran toward his house. As his hand took hold of the doorknob, Amelia spoke again.

"She's not there."

Billy spun around. "What are you talking about?"

"I'm so sorry...I thought you knew. Nobody's there."

Without taking his eyes off Amelia, Billy pointed at his driveway. "You see that car? That's my aunt's. She's inside the house."

"What car, Billy?"

Billy turned his head. There was nothing there. The snow was still sleek, fresh, and undisturbed.

"But how…"

Amelia now stood next to him. "We can't go home."

"What's going on?" Billy knew he should have felt frightened, or at least angry, but he felt nothing.

"They took me a couple of weeks before you. After I lost my teddy bear."

"*Nobody took me!*" Billy shouted angrily. It was the most emotion he had felt in almost a week.

"Are you cold?" Amelia asked.

Billy was about to respond, but then he noticed he did not feel the winter air at all. It was not due to his jacket, because he was not warm, either. He took off his hefty jacket and hat, but still nothing. He stood in the shin-deep snow in only his grey pajamas. He should have been freezing.

"What's going on? Why can't I feel *anything*?"

"There's nothing left to feel. We're dead."

"Dead?" Billy's head began to spin. "But how?"

"You know."

Billy did know. It had happened a week ago, but he had written it off as another nightmare. It was the night he unplugged his nightlight and decided not to check his closet twice. He was ten years old, after all. It was time to grow up. He had climbed into bed, and after a few moments of anxiety, he finally fell asleep.

His nightmare began instantaneously. His closet door creaked open, and something big came through. Billy hid under his covers, but to no avail. Whatever had come out of his closet threw his covers aside and grabbed his naked ankle. Billy screamed. From down the hall, he heard ruffling from his parents' room. They would not make it in time. The scaly hand tightened its grip and dragged Billy from his bed. He screeched, cried, and even lost control of his bladder. The creature pulled him into the closet and slammed the door shut behind them. The last thing Billy remembered was its musty breath inches from his face.

"It was only a dream," Billy said. He dropped to his knees.

"No, it wasn't," Amelia responded.

"But I woke up the next morning, in my bed!"

"So did I." Amelia patted him on the shoulder.

Billy stared down at the snow.

"There's more, Billy."

"Like what?"

"We're stuck here."

"What do you mean we're stuck?"

"There's some kind of force field that won't let us leave Turner Street."

"Force field? What?"

"I don't know how it works. You can try to leave for yourself and see what happens. But I've been trying since I died. There's no way past it."

Billy continued to stare at the snow. "What about my parents?"

"They went to stay with your grandmother," Amelia said. "My parents suggested it when they came over yesterday. It's what my parents did when I disappeared. And your aunt, she was never here."

"What?"

"Think about it, have you seen her since she got here?"

Billy was silent. He had not seen her. He had only assumed she was there. She always came over when his parents went out.

"What—What do we do now?"

"We don't really know."

"*We?*"

"All the other kids who disappeared."

"Where are they?"

"All over the place. Some are still in their rooms, and others are walking the street..." Amelia trailed off.

They stood in silence.

"So we're stuck here forever?"

"No, I think things will change soon," she continued. "Dennis, from a couple houses down, said the last thing he heard, was someone talking about a tree. And once it sprouts, *then* we'll have somewhere to go."

"A tree?"

"Yeah."

Billy nodded. "What do you think will happen when it sprouts?"

"Who knows? But it can't be any worse than this."

"What do we do till then?"

"You want to build another snowman?"

About the Author

R.S. Veira is an author, director, and dreamer. He is currently writing, directing, and dreaming at Dream With Me Productions in Los Angeles, California. To learn more about R.S. Veira and his writing, visit him at rsveira.com.